SUPERDOODLES

RAIN FOREST

WRITTEN AND ILLUSTRATED BY BEV ARMSTRONG

The Learning Works

The Learning Works

Designed and edited by
Sherri M. Butterfield

Copyright © 1993
The Learning Works, Inc.
Santa Barbara, California 93160

Library of Congress Catalog Number:
92-074101
ISBN 0-88160-218-3
LW 302

Printed in the United States of America.

Current Printing (last digit):
10 9 8 7 6 5 4 3 2 1

Introduction

SUPERDOODLES are books that provide simple, step-by-step instructions for super line drawings. The rain forest plants and animals in this book may be sketched large for murals or posters, or small for bookmarks and flip books. They may be used individually in separate pictures or combined to create a South American scene.

As you follow the steps, draw in pencil. Dotted lines appear in some steps. Make these lines light so that they can be easily erased later. When you have finished your drawing, erase all unnecessary lines. To give your drawing a finished look, go over the remaining lines with a colored pencil, crayon, or felt-tipped pen.

If you enjoy this book, look for other **Learning Works SUPERDOODLES**. Titles in this series include *Dinosaurs, Mammals, Sports,* and *Vehicles.*

basilisk lizard

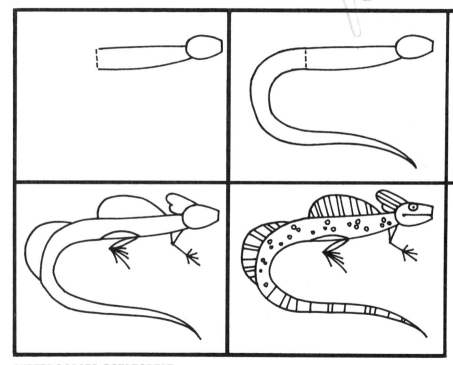

These big lizards can swim under water to escape from predators. Draw a swimming basilisk lizard. Add some fishes to your drawing.

bird-eating spider

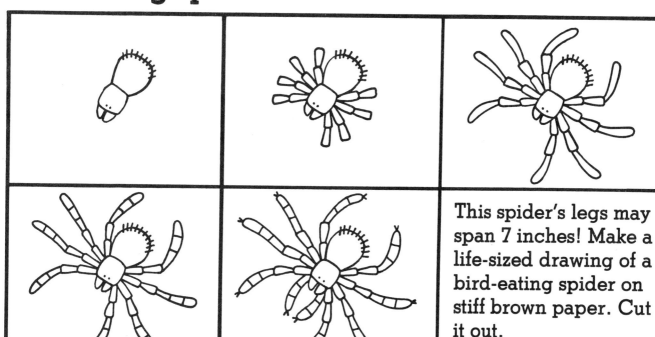

This spider's legs may span 7 inches! Make a life-sized drawing of a bird-eating spider on stiff brown paper. Cut it out.

brocket

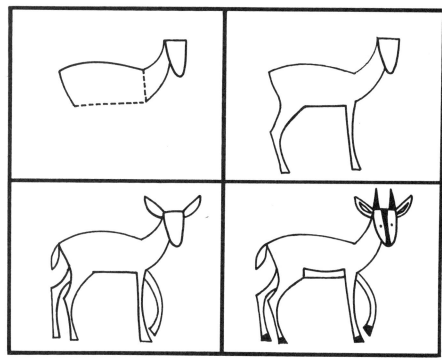

These shy little deer are about 2 feet tall at the shoulder. Draw a picture of yourself next to a brocket. How much taller are you than the brocket?

cock of the rock

These bright orange birds sometimes gather on the forest floor to "dance," hopping around and bowing to each other. Draw this scene.

curassow

This bird has a yellow beak with a strange lump on it. Draw a curassow that is walking along a branch, finding fruit or seeds to eat.

emerald tree boa

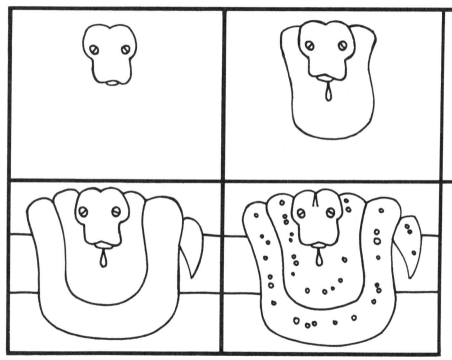

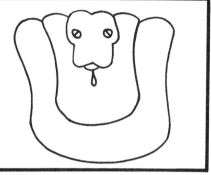

As adults, these boas are bright green with white spots. When young, they are reddish brown. How will you color your snake?

giant armadillo

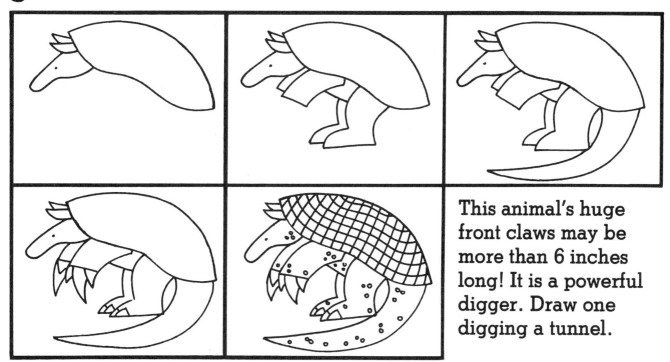

This animal's huge front claws may be more than 6 inches long! It is a powerful digger. Draw one digging a tunnel.

giant otter

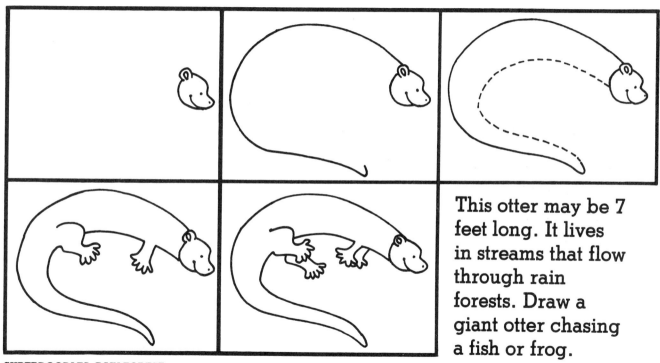

This otter may be 7 feet long. It lives in streams that flow through rain forests. Draw a giant otter chasing a fish or frog.

hoatzin

These large, wild-looking birds build nests of long sticks loosely piled together. Draw a hoatzin sitting on its nest.

horned frog

Using the picture you have drawn, make a poster encouraging people to learn more about rain forests.

hummingbird

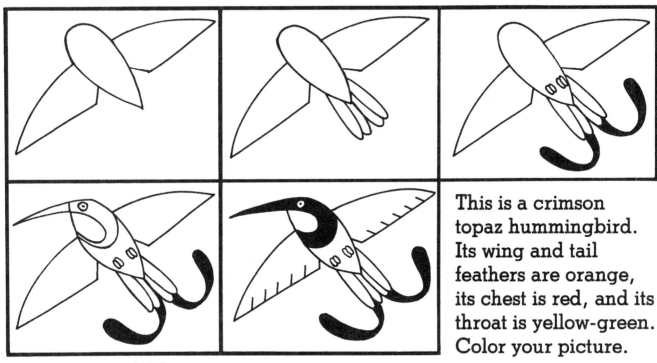

This is a crimson topaz hummingbird. Its wing and tail feathers are orange, its chest is red, and its throat is yellow-green. Color your picture.

katydid

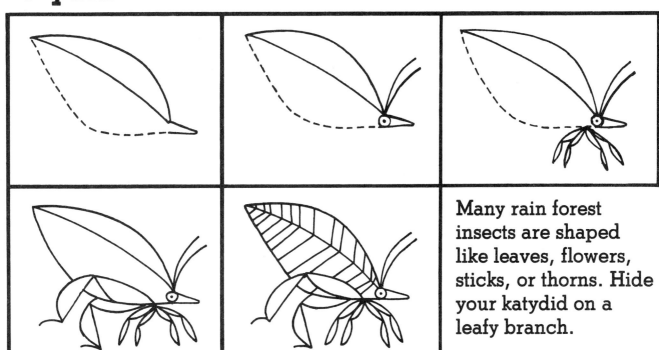

Many rain forest insects are shaped like leaves, flowers, sticks, or thorns. Hide your katydid on a leafy branch.

kinkajou

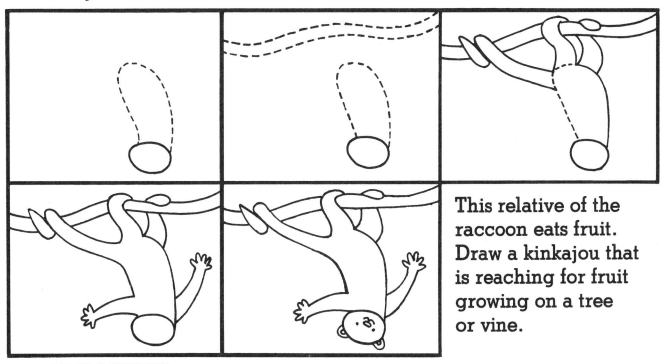

This relative of the raccoon eats fruit. Draw a kinkajou that is reaching for fruit growing on a tree or vine.

lantern fly

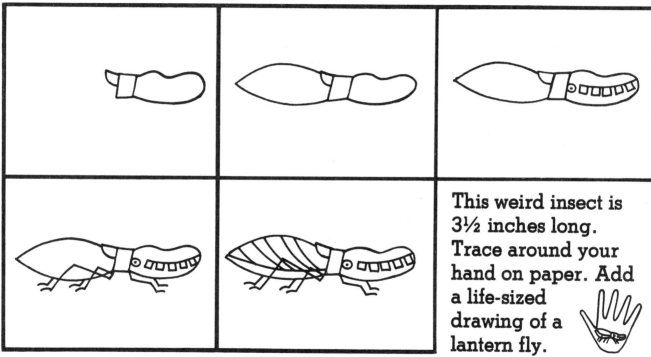

This weird insect is 3½ inches long. Trace around your hand on paper. Add a life-sized drawing of a lantern fly.

long-tongued bat

These bats drink nectar from flowers. Draw a flowering plant (see page 23) from which your bat may feed.

margay

The margay is just a little bigger than a domestic cat. Draw a margay that is stalking a bird or lizard.

marmosa

Newborn marmosas ride in their mothers' pouches. Older ones ride on their mothers' backs. Draw a marmosa with babies.

19

motmot

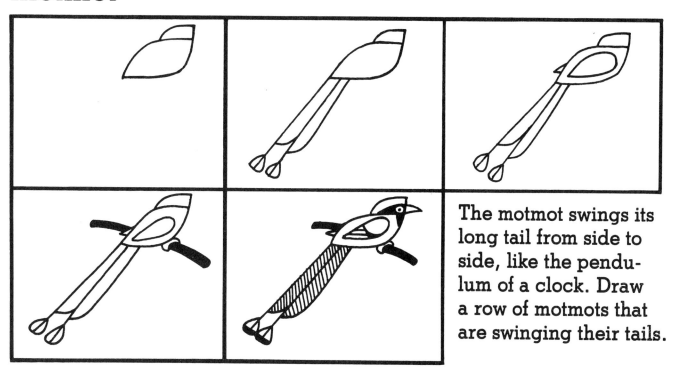

The motmot swings its long tail from side to side, like the pendulum of a clock. Draw a row of motmots that are swinging their tails.

parrot

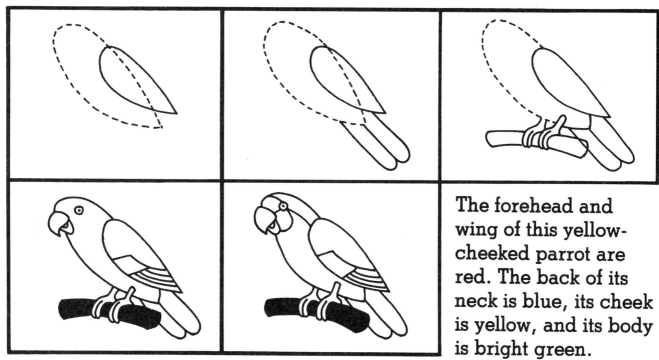

The forehead and wing of this yellow-cheeked parrot are red. The back of its neck is blue, its cheek is yellow, and its body is bright green.

peccary

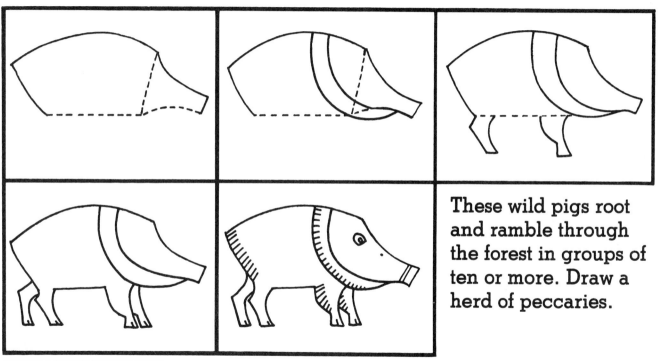

These wild pigs root and ramble through the forest in groups of ten or more. Draw a herd of peccaries.

plants

Rain forest plants include trees, ferns, vines, bushes, and mushrooms. Animals feed on their leaves, flowers, fruit, seeds, and nectar.

rhinoceros beetle

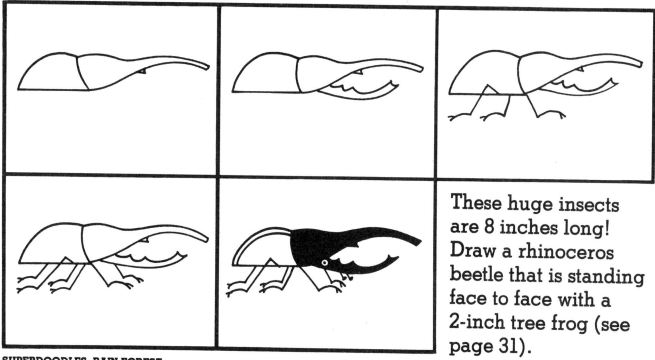

These huge insects are 8 inches long! Draw a rhinoceros beetle that is standing face to face with a 2-inch tree frog (see page 31).

scarlet ibis

Ibises are water birds. Draw one reflected in a river as shown. Use tracing paper to copy the bird upside down.

spider monkey

These lively monkeys live in groups. Draw a row of monkeys running along a branch. Picture each one's tail in a different position.

spoonbill

These birds wade in rain forest streams, catching small water animals with their oversized beaks. Give your spoonbill a stream to wade in.

tamandua

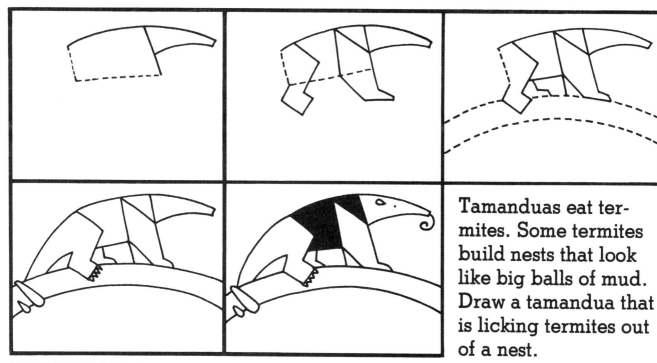

Tamanduas eat termites. Some termites build nests that look like big balls of mud. Draw a tamandua that is licking termites out of a nest.

three-toed sloth

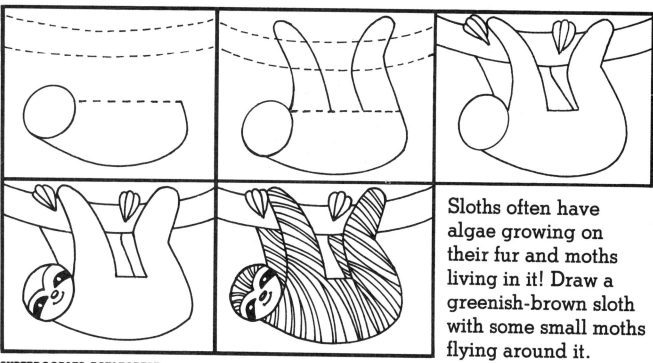

Sloths often have algae growing on their fur and moths living in it! Draw a greenish-brown sloth with some small moths flying around it.

SUPERDOODLES: RAIN FOREST
©1993—The Learning Works, Inc.

toucan

Toucans use their long beaks to pick fruit. They toss the fruit in the air, catch it, and swallow it. Draw a toucan that is eating.

tree frog

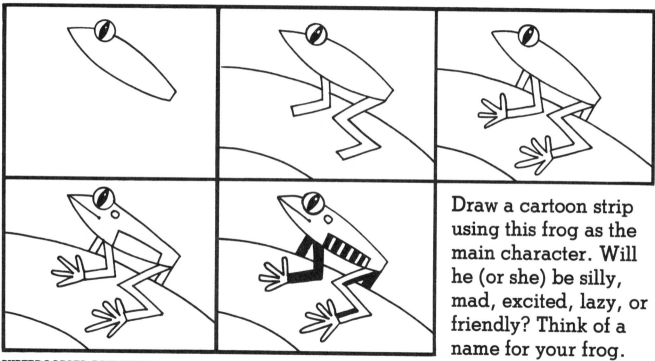

Draw a cartoon strip using this frog as the main character. Will he (or she) be silly, mad, excited, lazy, or friendly? Think of a name for your frog.

tropical fishes

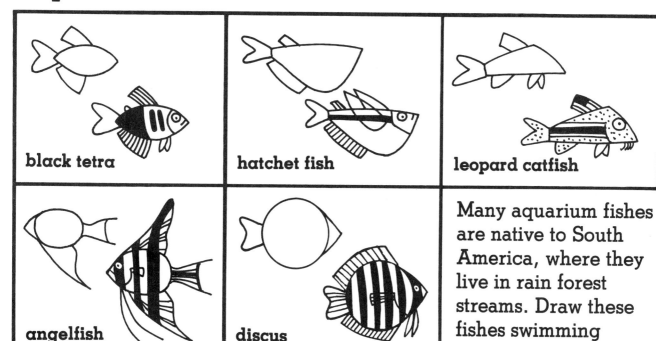

black tetra

hatchet fish

leopard catfish

angelfish

discus

Many aquarium fishes are native to South America, where they live in rain forest streams. Draw these fishes swimming among water plants.

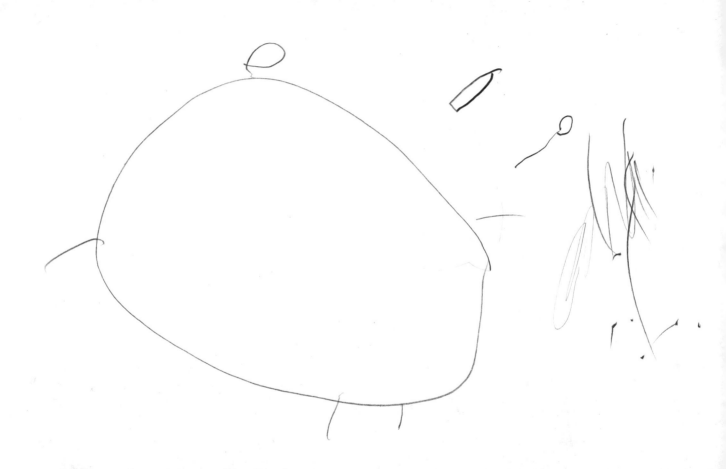